GRuBtoWN taLes

Book Two

The YeaR That I t RaiNed Cows

or

That Well-Known Secret Door

A bit about the author

Philip Ardagh is the award-winning author of the Eddie Dickens adventures, currently in over 30 languages. He wrote BBC radio's first truly interactive radio drama, collaborated with Sir Paul McCartney on his first children's book and is a 'regularly irregular' reviewer of children's books for the *Guardian*. Married with a son, he divides his time between Tunbridge Wells and Grubtown, where he cultivates his impressive beard.

Other children's books by Philip Ardagh published by Faber & Faber

GRuBtoWN taLes
Stinking Rich and Just Plain Stinky

FICTION FOR 8+
The Eddie Dickens Trilogy
Awful End
Dreadful Acts
Terrible Times
The Further Adventures of Eddie Dickens
Dubious Deeds
Horrendous Habits
Final Curtain
Unlikely Exploits
The Fall of Fergal
Heir of Mystery
The Rise of the House of McNally

High in the Clouds
with Paul McCartney & Geoff Dunbar

NON-FICTION
The Hieroglyphs Handbook
Teach Yourself Ancient Egyptian
The Archaeologist's Handbook
The Insider's Guide to Digging Up the Past
Did Dinosaurs Snore?
100½ Questions about Dinosaurs Answered
Why Are Castles Castle-Shaped?
100½ Questions about Castles Answered

GRuBtoWN taLes
Book Two

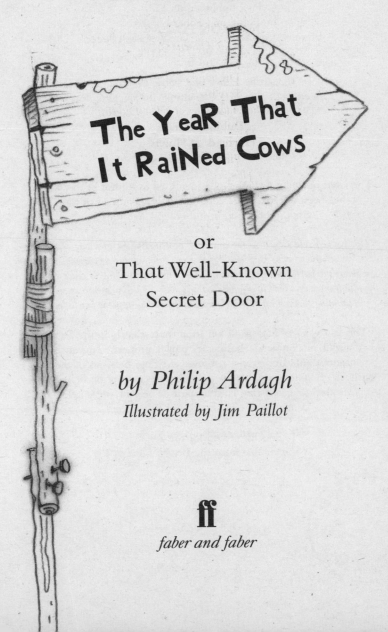

The YeaR That It RaiNed Cows

or
That Well-Known
Secret Door

by Philip Ardagh
Illustrated by Jim Paillot

ff
faber and faber

For Héloïse,
with love

First published in 2009
by Faber and Faber Limited
BloomsburyHouse, 74-77 Great Russell Street,
London WC1B 3DA

Typeset by Faber and Faber Limited
Printed in England by CPI BookMarque, Croydon

This is a work of fiction. Other than those clearly in the public
domain, all characters, businesses, places, properties, products,
organisations and even Grubtown itself are figments of the
author's imagination (with the possible exception of himself). Any
similarities to existing entities, past or present, are purely
coincidental and should not be inferred.

A CIP record for this book
is available from the British Library

ISBN 978-0-571-24233-7

2 4 6 8 10 9 7 5 3 1

A bit about Grubtown

You won't find Grubtown on any maps. The last time any map-makers were sent anywhere near the place they were found a week later wearing nothing but pages from a telephone directory, and calling for their mothers. It's certainly a town and certainly grubby – except for the squeaky-clean parts – but everything else we know about the place comes from Beardy Ardagh, town resident and author of these tales.

Grubtown Tales were made possible through the participation of the following people, animals and organisations:

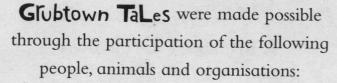

THE GRUBTOWN
CHAMBER OF COMMERCE

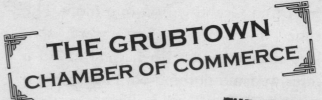

THE GRUBTOWN
CHAMBER OF
HORRORS

THE OFFICE
*of the Mayor
of Grubtown*

THE SHED
*of the Mayor
of Grubtown*

OFFAL'S
SUNBEDS

*The Mayor
of Grubtown
Himself*

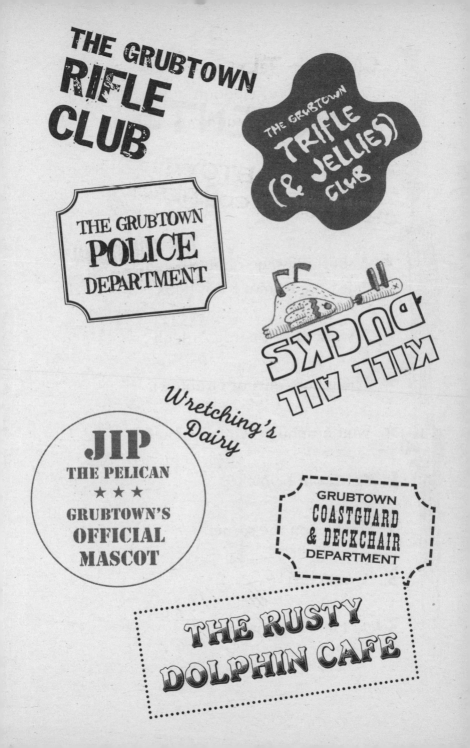

CONTENTS

These pages have been left blank
at the request of the author
in order to waste trees.

A short message about the paper we *didn't* use to make this book

The plan was to use trees from Grubtown Forest to make the paper for this book. That was the plan. Unfortunately, the author of **Grubtown TaLes**, Beardy Ardagh, had a serious falling out with Grubtown Forest's chief forester. Not just falling out as in 'having an argument' but also falling out as in 'falling out of an aeroplane'.

Fortunately for Beardy Ardagh, it was only Hardfast Tendril (the forester) who actually fell from a plane. Unfortunately for Beardy Ardagh, Hardfast Tendril accused him of

1

PUSHING him out. Beardy Ardagh denies this, which is why the two men fell out (in the argument sense).

Mr Ardagh isn't saying that he didn't hit Mr Tendril on the back with his hand, just that it was 'a friendly slap-on-the-back rather than a shove'. Hardfast Tendril sees it rather differently (from his hospital bed).

Beardy Ardagh has apologised for the accident but Hardfast Tendril has refused to 'let a single twig or leaf have anything to do with one of Beardy's stupid books'. So it's been printed on some different paper altogether. The paper that's now in your hands.

A word from
Beardy Ardagh

Those of you who've already read *Stinking Rich and Just Plain Stinky* will be familiar with most of the people who appear in this Grubtown Tale. Young Jilly Cheeter is back (though she's no longer Grubtown's resident duck-gatherer). Her friend Mango Claptrap is here again too (and he's still wearing his strangely short shorts). There's the mayor Flabby Gomez, the chief of police Grabby Hanson and – oh, yes – there's ME.

For those of you who don't already know me, SHAME ON YOU!!!! (Perhaps you've had your head stuck in a beehive for the past

I-don't-know-how-many-years, or were snatched by aliens and left stranded in the luggage hold of a spaceship?) I'm a life-loving (and very bearded) author and resident of Grubtown. And don't believe a word about my being a bit grumpy and rude sometimes. That's just a story made up by a bunch of knuckleheads who couldn't tie their own shoe-laces if they *had* lace-up shoes, which they don't. (They can only manage Velcro ones, and they even find those tricky to manage.) Enough said.

Enjoy *The Year That It Rained Cows*. It is a work of true genius.

Beardy Ardagh ●

Grubtown

The inhabitants
of Grubtown

At the back of the book (starting on page 123), you'll find a list of some of the people who live in Grubtown, including Jilly Cheeter and Mango Claptrap but NOT Hardfast Tendril, for obvious reasons. If he's going to upset me — I mean that lovely Mr Ardagh — with those false accusations about a friendly back-slap being a shove, he can't expect to be included, now, can he?

Wait a minute! Wait a minute! I asked you a question!

*C*an he?
Oh, never mind. Let's get this story started . . .

Chapter One
Watch out below!

It started with the freakiest of freak accidents: a man on a bike being flattened by a cow that fell from the sky. It happened a few summers back, outside The Rusty Dolphin cafe. Grabby Hanson, Grubtown's chief of police, was the first on the scene. (He'd been enjoying a bacon sandwich in the cafe when he heard an extraordinary **FLWUMPH** followed by a startled '**Moo!**')

9

Running outside, he found the man and the bike both under that cow I just mentioned. And I don't care if you don't believe me because it's true.

'Are you all right under there?' he asked Limbo Goulash, who was the man in question.

'It came out of nowhere!' groaned Mr Goulash. 'It fell from the sky!'

Hanson unclipped his police radio from his

shiny black police belt and muttered a few police words into it. Moments later, Constable Gelatine came out of the cafe wiping a milky foam moustache from his (policeman's) top lip with the back of his hand.

'What is it, Chief?' he asked.

Grabby Hanson nodded in the direction of the cow on the man on the bike. 'Fell from the sky,' he said.

'Both of them?' asked Constable Gelatine.

'Just the cow.'

'Are you all right, Limbo?' asked Grabby Hanson. Funnily enough, he'd climbed through an open window into Limbo's house and taken a few of his things just a couple of days before. (Our chief of police is forever stealing things, but he always, *always* gives them back.)

'I'm a bit squashed,' said Limbo Goulash. 'Any chance of getting it off me?' He felt short of breath and his ribs hurt.

'I'll do my best,' said Grabby Hanson, 'but I don't know much about cows.'

'Me neither,' admitted Constable Gelatine. 'I reckon we'll either have to pull from the front or push from the back.'

'Good thinking, Gelatine,' said Grabby Hanson.

'What about a carrot?' suggested a voice from among the on-lookers now gathering around the fringes of the accident. It belonged to Luminous Shard who was wiping his filthy hands on his favourite dirty mechanic's cloth.

'What *about* a carrot?' asked Constable Gelatine.

'I mean, couldn't you wave a carrot in front of her face?' said Shard.

'How do you know it's a she?' asked Grabby Hanson.

'All cows are shes.'

'You have a point there,' admitted the chief of police. 'And, no, I don't think cows eat carrots.'

'You're probably thinking of donkeys, Luminous,' said Limbo Goulash from his position (flat astride the bicycle) under the cow. He was on good terms with Luminous Shard since the mechanic had managed to fix the lawnmower he'd been left by a distant cousin.

'Shouldn't someone call a doctor?' said Jilly

Cheeter, a girl who had been fishing off the jetty with her friend Mango Claptrap when they'd heard the '**FLWUMPH -Moo!**' and come to see what was going on. (Jilly and Mango are about the same age, but she always looks older because he's a bit smaller and will insist on wearing shorts.)

'A doctor?' said Chief of Police Grabby Hanson. 'An excellent idea!'

'I'm not so sure . . .' said Limbo Goulash. 'Doctors are expensive.'

'Then why not send for Dr Fraud?' Mango Claptrap suggested.

'Good thinking!' said Goulash and Hanson at almost exactly the same time.

(Dr Fraud is the cheapest doctor here in Grubtown. That's probably because he's not a real doctor, but he's very popular with his patients. Even those of them who've died in his care have never said a word against him afterwards.)

While they waited for Dr Fraud to arrive, everyone joined in helping first to push and then to pull the cow. She wouldn't budge.

'Perhaps she's injured too,' said Luminous Shard. 'After all, she did fall from the sky.'

'Then again, she landed on something fairly soft,' said Limbo Goulash. 'Me.'

'Good point.' Luminous Shard nodded. A great big pink tongue suddenly flicked out of the cow's mouth and began licking the top of Shard's (totally bald) head.

'Cows like salt,' said Mango Claptrap, who knows all sorts of strange things. 'It must be your sweat she's after.' It was a hot sunny day.

'Actually, it feels rather nice,' said Luminous Shard. The headache he'd had all morning – not helped by the loud **'FLWUMPH-Moo!'** a short while back – was suddenly feeling a lot better.

Dr Fraud stepped out of his sleek black motorcar and hurried over, clutching his

impressive-looking doctor's bag. 'Where's the patient?' he asked.

'He's the one under the cow,' said Jilly Cheeter, raising her eyebrows.

'Of course,' nodded Dr Fraud. He bent down next to Limbo Goulash. 'How are you doing, Limbo?'

'I can't feel my legs,' said Goulash.

'And what would you want to feel your legs for anyway?' asked Dr Fraud. 'I've been out and about all day and I haven't stopped to feel my legs once. Feeling my top pocket to check I've got my eye-glasses? Yes. Feeling my trouser pockets to check I've got my keys? Yes. But feeling my legs? Never.'

'He's right you know!' said Mrs Awning, who was now standing immediately behind Mango Claptrap and Jilly Cheeter. If there was an accident to be had, it was usually she who was slap-bang in the middle of it. *Not* to be the injured one must have been an unusual feeling for her.

She turned suddenly and poked herself in the eye with the end of Mango's homemade fishing rod.

'Ouch!' she yelped.

There. Much better.

Chapter Two
Flabby's on the scene

'I think it would be best if we got the cow off Goulash,' announced Dr Fraud.

'We've been trying, doc,' said Constable Gelatine, clearly hurt that the pretend-doctor thought that *they* hadn't thought of that.

'Good. Then keep trying. I think that would be better than any course of action I could take at present.' Dr Fraud may be a fraud but he always talks like a true professional. (Perhaps that's because he's a professional fraud.)

'Where do you think she came from?' Mango Claptrap asked Jilly Cheeter.

'The cow?'

He nodded. They both looked up into the sunny clear-blue sky to see if there were any clues. A few seagulls wheeled about overhead. There was no sign of anything out of the ordinary.

'The lighthouse is too far away,' said Mango, looking across to Grubtown's familiar red-and-white striped landmark.

'And how would the cow have got up all those winding steps in the first place?' added Jilly Cheeter.

'Exactly,' said Mango Claptrap.

It turned out that no one had heard an engine noise: no whooshing of jets, no whirring of propellers and no rat-a-tat-tat of helicopter rotor-blades. At that stage, in the back of his mind, Grabby Hanson was thinking that the cow must have been dropped – or fallen – from a glider or hot-air balloon.

'**Woooah!**' said Limbo Goulash. 'I think she's leaking!'

Chief Grabby Hanson took a look. 'You're all right,' he said. 'It's milk coming from her udder.'

Limbo Goulash was relieved. Of all the liquids that might be seeping from an injured cow and covering him, this was the one that bothered him the least

'Why don't you call up Barton Wretching, Mr Hanson?' Jilly suggested. 'He probably knows more about cows than most people in Grubtown.'

Grabby Hanson was impressed. The reason why Barton Wretching probably knows more about cows than most people in town is that he's one of the few people who actually has any. He owns a herd and runs *Wretching's Dairy*, named after his mother, Clam

Wretching, who founded the business. She handed it over to him on her ninetieth birthday then retired to bed. (She's still there now. I checked. I didn't wake her.) If the cow hadn't fallen from above, and had simply been running loose, Grabby Hanson would automatically have assumed that she belonged to Barton Wretching. There was even a picture of a cow on the *Wretching's Dairy* ice-cream tubs and on the milk cartons that grace just about every breakfast table in Grubtown, except for the unlikeable Fox family's.

Constable Gelatine was sent to fetch Mr Wretching. Luminous Shard, meanwhile, had managed to get hold of a rope.

He went to tie it around the cow's neck. Then stopped. 'Does anyone know any knots?' he asked.

Mango Claptrap was about to reveal that he knew some of the very knottiest of knots when a large shadow appeared over the proceedings. It belonged to Mayor Flabby Gomez, which made it a very large (and very flabby) shadow indeed, shaped a bit like a bag of badgers.

'What appears to be the problem?' he asked.

Flabby Gomez is not only the mayor but he also *owns* Grubtown, having won it from his father, Big Man Gomez, in a raffle. For some reason, he was standing in front of them with Jip – the town's pelican mascot – under his arm.

'This cow fell out of the sky and landed on Limbo Goulash and his bicycle, Mr Mayor,' said Chief Hanson.

'It's not my bike,' said Goulash, now soaked in milk.

'Whose is it, then?' asked Grabby Hanson, with interest. He wondered whether Goulash had *stolen* it. Grabby Hanson hates thieves. They give people-who-take-things a bad name.

'Marley Gripe's,' said Goulash. (Gripe is the town's sign-painter. He even painted the sign for **THE RUSTY DOLPHIN**, lettering, dolphin and all.)

'And does Marley know you have it?'

'Of course, Grabby.'

'Okay. Fine.'

'Don't you think you should get out from under there, Limbo? You're blocking the free-flow of –' He looked around. There was no traffic. '– of town life,' he said.

On the word 'life', Mayor Flabby Gomez slapped the cow's rump with his hand. It stopped licking Luminous Shard's head, let out an irritated 'Moo!' and moved off Limbo Goulash.

Shard looked down at the milk-sodden rather flat-looking Limbo Goulash, and went to help him up.

'Everyone leave him be,' instructed Dr Fraud. 'I must give him a thorough examination before we risk moving him.'

'Fair enough, doc,' said Flabby, with the wave of a hand, the other still clutching Jip. 'See you all later.' The mayor strode off down towards *The Crooked Sixpence*, an illegal gambling ship permanently moored off shore, in the shadow of the lighthouse.

He was humming a happy tune.

Chapter Three
'On ya bike!'

As far as Jilly Cheeter and Mango Claptrap could see, Dr Fraud's thorough examination of Limbo Goulash consisted of him prodding his patient just about everywhere and seeing when and where he said '**Ouch!**' the loudest. It seemed quite a good method.

'I think you've probably got a few cracked ribs and you'll have some nasty bruises in the morning but otherwise you're fine. Then again, you might want to ask a proper doctor,' said Fraud.

Goulash thought of the large bill that would land him. 'No thanks, Dr Fraud. Your word is good enough for me.'

Jilly Cheeter and Mango Claptrap picked up the bike Mr Goulash had borrowed from Marley Gripe.

'The bike looks fine,' announced Mango Claptrap.

'Oh no,' said Limbo Goulash. Dr Fraud was busy bandaging his chest.

'What is it?' asked the fake doctor.

'I promised Marley that he'd have his bike back by now.'

'We can take it,' said Jilly, who doesn't have a bike of her own.

'Thank you,' said Limbo Goulash.

Which is how Jilly Cheeter came to be riding Marley Gripe's bicycle with Mango Claptrap sitting on the handlebars, holding both of their fishing rods. I'm not sure they'd allow that where you live. It isn't the safest mode of transp –

‒ *THUMP!* Oh dear. The first time they veered off the road on to the pavement they fell about laughing. (This was outside Offal's Sunbeds.) The second time, it wasn't so funny. The third time they hit a lamppost near Kill All Ducks, a shop owned by the Fox family who have a thing against ducks. Why? Because a duck's quack caused Mrs Fox to lose her concentration during a driving test, drive off the end of a jetty and on to the deck of a passing ferry. Or so they claimed. Lately, they were in dispute with just about everyone over everything. So much so that the local newspapers[*] had stopped printing their letters. They wanted to allow space for other residents to moan.

Marley Gripe lives inland, on the outskirts of town, so Mango and Jilly cycled along the river walk, which runs along the bottom of the garden of what had once been the home of TV chef Hybrid Byword.

[*] *The Grubtown Daily Herald* and *The Grubtown Weekly Gerald*

Hybrid Byword is possibly the most famous person to come out of Grubtown. (I wasn't actually born here, so can't include myself.) If you've never heard of him, you must come from another planet, so 'Welcome to Earth, stranger!' As if you need telling that Hybrid Byword is probably the most famous television chef in the history of television chefs *ever*. There are chefs you see on television and in magazines and newspapers almost every day of the week, but not one of them comes close to being as famous as Hybrid Byword (not even Frizzle Sweary-Man). He is the always-and-forever KING of the television chefs.

The person who now lived in Byword's mansion kept himself very much to himself. He was rarely seen by anybody and when he did venture out, he wore tinted green spectacles and an (obviously) false white wizard beard (like something out of an amateur production of *Hairy Feet and the Magic Ring*). He called himself Ronald Brown – which most townsfolk thought was a ridiculous name if ever they'd heard one, and was obviously as fake as his beard – and many rumours grew up about him.

One such rumour was that he was the missing drummer from the pop group Not So Good When Playing Live who'd had a number of hit songs, but performed rubbish concerts. Another was that he was a retired spy, though I never thought that was likely because his disguise was so bad. For a while it seemed to be fashionable to think that he was the exiled King of

Tonk but this proved to be untrue when the real King of Tonk turned out to be living in a left-luggage locker somewhere in South America.

The truth be told, I don't think anyone really cared who 'Ronald Brown' was, so long as he didn't throw loud parties and was more interesting than the 'Ronald Brown' he pretended to be.

Jilly and Mango found Marley Gripe in his studio – a small converted brick outhouse – when they arrived. He had got as far as painting the '**PURPLE OU**' of '**PURPLE OUTING'S MUSIC SHACK**'.

'What do you want?' he asked in his usual grumpy tone.

'We're returning your bike,' said Mango.

'And what are you doing with my bicycle in the first place?' demanded Marley Gripe, carefully putting down his paint brush. 'It's not for Limbo Goulash to be lending it out to the likes of you.'

'What's wrong with the likes of us?' asked Mango Claptrap.

'He means children, don't you, Mr Gripe?' said Jilly.

The sign-painter muttered something they couldn't understand.

'Anyway,' said Jilly, 'Mr Goulash got flattened by a falling cow, so we said we'd bring your bike back –'

'A falling cow?' muttered Marley Gripe. 'A likely story!'

Chapter Three-and-a-half
Half a chapter

There are just two local newspapers in Grubtown* and Limbo Goulash and the falling cow was front-page news in – or should that be *on*? – both. There were interviews with a number of on-lookers and with Grabby Hanson – who managed to steal one reporter's pen and the other reporter's pair of green-felt trousers, without either noticing, and was on the verge of arresting himself when he returned the items before publication.

**The Grubtown Daily Herald* and
The Grubtown Weekly Gerald

Luminous Shard was quoted as saying how the cow's licky tongue had helped cure him of his very bad headache, and there was a photo of Mrs Awning wearing an eye-patch after the jab from the tip of the fishing rod. (She also had her arm in a sling from when she'd slipped on a highly polished hospital floor.) Then there was the large picture of the cow 'being cared for by staff at Wretching's Dairy until its rightful owner is found'.

The one noticeable absence from the reports in both papers was Limbo Goulash. There were no comments from him or photos of him after the accident. The reason for this? He was hoping that the two rival newspapers would both offer him GREAT BIG BAGS OF MONEY to tell his story to their particular paper. He was waiting to see who would promise the most

He had a long wait.

A very long wait.

A very, *very* long wait.

If you think that a piece of very long string is long, then you should see just how long Limbo Goulash's very long wait was.

As it turned out, he eventually sold his whole exclusive story for a family-size pack of Swedish meatballs from Reynard's Food Emporium (with the sell-by date blacked out with a thick black felt-tip pen). By then there was a much bigger story of *international* importance to report.

There'll be more about that.

Later.

Chapter Four
A really bad sign

The way I wrote about Marley Gripe a little earlier on may make him out to be a bit of a grump-bag, and he doesn't come across too brilliantly in this next part either. It's therefore important for you to know that I've got nothing against him, *even if I have good reason to.*

In all the time I've lived in Grubtown, I've only ever known Marley Gripe make one serious mistake with a sign and that was one he made for me for my front gate.

The sign was supposed to read:

CLEAR OFF.

UNINVITED VISITORS UNWELCOME.

JUST BECAUSE I'M AT HOME DOESN'T MEAN

THAT I'M NOT WORKING. I'M AN AUTHOR.

I NEED PEACE AND QUIET.

When he proudly unveiled it, however, it actually read:

PAY PHONE BILL BY FRIDAY

I was furious for six good reasons:

1. Because he'd painted completely the wrong sign.

2. Because I'd written the wording for the sign on the back of one of my 'must do' notes and given it to Marley Gripe (instead of sticking it on the fridge door), I'd forgotten to pay the phone bill (which explained why the phone was no longer working).

3. I had a sneaking suspicion that Marley *knew* that he'd gone for the wording on the wrong side of the paper, but I couldn't prove it.

4. I'd already paid two-thirds of the money up front 'for materials'.

5. I was still without a sign on my front gate reading:

CLEAR OFF.
UNINVITED VISITORS UNWELCOME.
JUST BECAUSE I'M AT HOME DOESN'T MEAN
THAT I'M NOT WORKING. I'M AN AUTHOR.
I NEED PEACE AND QUIET.

6. Er, okay, that should have been *five* reasons. I miscounted.

So I was upset, but that's not enough reason to start spreading lies about the man, now is it? If I had bad feelings towards Marley Gripe, I've got over them. If I make him seem not-so nice, it's *because* he's not-so nice . . .

The day after the cow flattened Limbo Goulash, Gripe was using his bicycle to deliver

the newly completed sign – which Jilly
Cheeter and Mango Claptrap had seen him
working on – to **PURPLE OUTING'S
MUSIC SHACK**. Purple and his wife
Hind-Leg (who originally came from the
nearby village of Werty) have more children
than anyone else in Grubtown. Probably more
children than anyone else on the planet. I've
no idea how many children they have. I'm not

sure they do. I suspect the only person who knows just how many young Outings there are is our local know-all Informative Boothe and he's not telling. (Knowledge is power and porridge is oats, remember.)

Fortunately for Purple, he doesn't have to work for a living. He can feed all those (however-many) mouths without doing an honest day's labour. Why? Because in the

same raffle that Flabby Gomez won Grubtown and Sonia Pipkin won a container lorry full of doll's-house furniture, Purple Outing won a few acres of stinging nettles. It was down near the river walk, and had a fallen-down corrugated-iron shack in the middle of it.

But it was what he later discovered *under* that patch of ground that made him rich. If you're thinking oil or gold or stuff like that, you couldn't be further from the truth, so stop being such a smarty-pants and shuffle off in SHAME. For under that land he discovered Hybrid's Hoard.

As you ALL know by now, Hybrid Byword was the greatest of the great TV chefs. Near the end of his career, before he went a bit funny and started saying all that stuff about crows, Byword invented or created or concocted (or whatever it is chefs do) the most fabulous-tasting cake-based pudding in the whole history of the world. Presidents, royals, snobs, jackanapes and guttersnipes all clamoured and jostled to get so much as a tiny bite of the stuff. Rival chefs and food companies tried every trick in the book — and made up some new tricks especially — to try to get their hands on the recipe. They all failed.

And there was something even more incredible about this cake-based pudding than the fabulous taste alone. It never went off. If you were having a dinner party, you could plan ahead and buy it seventeen years in advance and it would still be fresh.

But, when the greatest TV chef of all time died, he took the secret of Byword's Pudding with him . . . so no one knew how to make it for themselves. Scientists pored over any remaining pieces that they could lay their hands on. Governments and food manufacturers called in molecular scientists and, to cut an already long story short, no one succeeded in coming up with anything that tasted or lasted like the original.

Pieces of the pud changed hands for SUPER-MASSIVE sums of money on Internet auction sites. Secret deals were made between top restaurants and between rival governments. Eventually, there were only half-a-dozen or so pieces known to remain, and four of them were in museums.

Then all of this changed. What did Purple Outing find under his recently won property? A rusty box containing Hybrid Byword's secret recipe? NO, I say, NO! And NO again!

What Purple discovered was a secret door leading to an enormous cavern: a cavern filled from top to bottom with what the world's media came to call Hybrid's Hoard: thousands of tonnes of Byword's Pudding. He'd been stockpiling it – hoarding it away – for reasons we may never know. So now

Purple Outing is the *second* most famous person to come out of Grubtown and certainly one of the richest. (Though not as rich as a squeaky-clean bald chap called Manual Org who lives in a tree off the Flimsy Bridge Road.)

Purple owns and runs **PURPLE OUTING'S MUSIC SHACK** because there's nothing else he'd rather do. He likes music. He likes talking to his customers – and those who just swing by to say, 'Hi!' – and he likes to hum and stare into space thinking about nothing in particular.

Marley Gripe hadn't asked Purple for two-thirds of the money up front for materials when he agreed to paint *his* new sign. He knew he'd get paid.

'It's great,' said Purple, admiring Gripe's handiwork. 'How much do I owe you?'

The sign-writer stated a ridiculously large amount of money.

Purple Outing laughed. 'I never agreed to that,' he said.

'Why not just give it to me, Purple?' said Marley Gripe. 'You can easily afford it.' (See? That's not a very nice thing to say.)

'That's not the point,' said Purple. 'We agreed a pr–'

He was interrupted by a terrifying crash and bits of ceiling plaster coming down on top of them. They dashed outside.

Marley Gripe's jaw dropped. Purple Outing simply gawked. There, sticking up from the roof of his beloved Music Shack was a life-size model of a cow.

Chapter Five
From bad to even badder still

Mango's dad, Furl Claptrap, came out of the Grubtown General Store & Post Office with two brand-new bumper word-search puzzle books a matter of minutes after this second – artificial – cow had hit the Music Shack. He was so excited at the thought of tackling some new puzzles that he barely took in what was going on around him.

Grabby Hanson was already on the scene. He was talking to Marley Gripe.

'First a cow lands on your bike while it's being ridden by Limbo Goulash and now a model cow lands on Purple's music shop while you're inside. You are what we in the police service call a common denominator.'

'It's what *I* call a coincidence,' snapped Gripe. 'Do you think a falling cow would recognise my bike from above?'

'You have a point,' our chief of police readily agreed, 'but I'm not a great believer in coincidences.'

'What about that year when lots of people bought you identical ties for your birthday?' asked Purple Outing.

'The ties were going cheap in a sale at Margo's,' said Grabby Hanson. 'No coincidence there, just people saving a little money.'

'Oh,' said Purple, reddening a little. He'd been one of the tie-buyers and he had indeed taken it from a 'bargain tie tub' near the

entrance to Margo's multi-purpose store.

'Hi, Dad,' said Mango Claptrap, who'd been on his way to try to find Jilly Cheeter.

'Hello, Mango,' said his dad.

'Wow!' said Mango. He'd just spotted the cow on Purple Outing's roof.

'Yeah,' said Furl Claptrap. 'Things are getting weirder and weirder around here. Nobody heard a thing – apart from the CRASH – and no sign of a plane either.'

Mango found a better position to look at the model cow. After a while, he said: 'It has the same markings.'

'What do you mean?' asked his dad.

'This cow has the same markings as the real cow that landed on Mr Goulash,' said Mango.

'Yup,' said Furl Claptrap, who'd seen the (black and white) photos of the cow in the paper. 'They're both black and white.'

'I don't mean that,' said Mango. 'I mean that the splodges on this cow have been painted to look exactly like the splodges on the real cow.'

'You sure?' asked Grabby Hanson, overhearing them talk.

'Absolutely. And a cow's markings are as individual as fingerprints,' said Mango with obvious pride. He'd read that on the back of a milk carton. ('Wretching's Dairy Fact No. 232', apparently.)

'You seem to know an awful lot about cows,' said the chief of police. 'And this cow in particular . . .'

'Are you suggesting that my Mango is somehow mixed up in all of this?' demanded Furl Claptrap, putting a large, protective (and impressively tattooed) arm around his son.

'I'm just grateful that there's someone as smart as your boy around when I need him. This case has suddenly got even more interesting.'

'It's a *case*?' asked Mango, glowing with pride.

'With the second – artificial – falling cow made to look like the first, and the criminal damage to Purple Outing's Music Shack roof? You bet it's a case. It's at the top of my Things-To-Do List.'

Mango couldn't wait to tell Jilly Cheeter.

Chapter Six
'Watch the skies!'

Mayor Flabby Gomez did what he did best. He formed an emergency committee and immediately called an emergency Emergency Committee Meeting. It was behind closed doors, or would have been if one of the double doors to the committee room hadn't got jammed half-open by an enormous piece of chewing gum stuck to the floor.

There was only one thing on the agenda at that first emergency meeting – apart from trying to shift that sticky piece of gum – and that was the falling cows.

'Do you think there'll be another one, Grabby?' asked Flabby Gomez from his place at the head of the table, seated in his extra-large chair. On the wall immediately behind him was an oil painting of his father, the late Big Man Gomez, picking his nose. Big Man Gomez often used to pick his nose very publicly just to prove to himself that there was no one who would dare ask him not to. He was that kind of person. (There's a word for it. Unpleasant.)

'Another falling cow, Mr Mayor?' said Grabby Hanson. 'Who knows? But if there is, we'll be ready. We're watching the skies.'

As far as I'm aware, there's only one sky (stretching around the whole world, helping to create a pretty fabulous atmosphere, if you ask me) but 'Watching the skies' (plural: *more than one*) sounds more dramatic than 'Watching the sky' (singular: *boring and alone*), doesn't it? And, being a good chief of police, Grabby Hanson is certainly a good showman.

And he did have plenty of people looking upwards, whether it be at the skies or sky. Townsfolk were clamouring to help.

Camshaft Thrift of The Rusty Dolphin supplied tea and coffee to the sky-watchers.

Minty Glibb of Minty's Cake Shop supplied end-of-day buns. Sonia Pipkin, local builder, supplied ladders for people wanting to climb up to high places. No one was allowed to use his lighthouse as a lookout tower because it was against coastguard regulations, but the lighthouse keeper, Garlic Hamper, promised to be extra, *extra* alert. (He gave the lenses of his binoculars an extra thorough clean.)

The only people who'd been really unwilling to take part were the Fox family. Mr and Mrs Fox appeared to be hiding, and Shaun, Garrideb, Mantle and Fastbuck complained that they had far more important things to do with their time, then slunk off.

While the chief was at the special meeting, Constable Gelatine was in charge of the sky-watch. He had us on roofs, in clearings and up trees, all with eyes peeled.

I myself don't have a head for heights but,

being tall, allowed
Condo Blotch to
stand on my
shoulders for a
better view during
her half-hour break
between cleaning
jobs. She'd borrowed
an old telescope
from somewhere.

Mrs Awning was
another of the
townsfolk who
volunteered her time
for the task and
wouldn't take 'No,
please go away and
leave us alone, Mrs
A. You're bound to
have another of
your accidents!' for

an answer. Unfortunately, with one eye under a patch and one arm in a sling, she lost her footing when trying to clamber up the telegraph pole she'd chosen, and ended up (face down) on the roof of Rambo Sanskrit's passing camper van. (Rather than call an ambulance, he simply left her on the roof of the van and drove straight to the hospital.)

Somehow the Grumbly girls were able to sky-watch and write a song about it at the same time. They called it '**Even Though We're Sky-Watching We've Somehow Found Time To Write This Song**' and it became a real favourite in the family. It includes that memorable line: '*I wonder hows/We're gonna stop them fallin' cows*' and is an impressive twenty-two verses long.

As luck would have it, it was Jilly Cheeter and Mango Claptrap who spotted something flying overhead. They were on official sky-watching duty up the big tree in Really Little

More Than a Patch of Grass With a Big Tree in it Park (which is really little more than a patch of grass with a big tree in it, not that far from Flimsy Bridge Road).

There was no engine sound of any kind and, whatever it was, it was moving in a graceful arc, inland from the direction of the sea.

'What on earth is it?' gasped Mango Claptrap.

'Whatever it is,' said Jilly Cheeter, 'it's coming this way.'

Sure enough, what started as a **dot,** got bigger . . .

. . . and bigger . . .

. . . and bigger . . .

. . . and bigger . . .

. . . and so on (you get the picture) . . .

until they could clearly see that it was:

another COW!

Chapter Seven
A trifle tragic

The third cow caused the most damage. It completely destroyed what was on the verge of being the biggest jelly trifle Grubtown – or, possibly, the world – had ever seen. The previous summer, in order to promote the change of The Duck House – home to ducks – into the Grubtown Museum, the town had hosted **THE WORLD BEATERS' FESTIVAL**. Like so many ideas, this had been the mayor's. The festival lasted a week during which the townsfolk had tried to break as many world records as possible.

The attempt to cook the world's largest omelette resulted in sixteen people getting very upset tummies from uncooked eggs. The attempt to break the record for the number of people fitting inside a particularly small brand of car resulted in a broken collar bone and a wedding. The weight-lifting was even more of a disaster, with one of the spectators — Mrs Awning — narrowly avoiding being struck by a runaway weight . . . only to be accidentally trampled by a passing angry mob. (The mob got even more angry as a result.

They hadn't been wearing the right kind of shoes for trampling, and that made them furious.) As for the sewing-while-sky-diving, the largest unsupported circle of people dressed as farmyard animals, and the yak-shearing competitions, you just don't want to know. Trust me. The two local papers* had a field day. The list of disasters was endless. Only the string-of-sausages tug-of-war was deemed a success, until Camshaft Thrift (owner of The Rusty Dolphin) was accused of cheating. The World-Beaters' Festival was an embarrassing blot on a town used to embarrassing blots, but not quite such big (blotchy) ones.

And what has this history to do with the jelly trifle in the public car park around the back of Fringe Street? Two words: Minty Glibb. Yes, the owner of **Minty's Cake Shop** was supposed to have been making world's biggest jelly trifle at the festival but had been locked in a basement instead. The locker-inner had been Mrs Johnson (formerly Miss Leggy Prune) as a protest over her husband – Mickey 'Steamroller' Johnson – being in prison for flattening **MINTY'S CAKE SHOP** and for attempting to flatten Minty herself in a dispute over a jam-filled doughnut. (Leggy had married Mickey in a special ceremony held in the jail.)

Anyway, though the festival was little more than an embarrassing memory of yesteryear, the record was still there to be broken, and Minty Glibb was in the process of attempting it . . . until the third cow (another fake one) landed in it with a terrible SPLAT. The result was trifle everywhere. And I mean everywhere. People were finding bits of it in their ear or hair or handbag or bumper word-search puzzle book for weeks afterwards. Those in the ISZ – Immediate Splat Zone – as Mayor Gomez officially designated it, were covered in jelly and cream and fruit segments and sponge fingers in a BIG way. It wasn't a pretty sight (though the red strawberry jelly did look rather nice in the sunlight).

This third (pretend) cow had the same markings as the other two, but was a little bit smaller than the second model cow which, in turn, had been a little bit smaller than the real one (who'd landed on Limbo Goulash).

Grabby Hanson was getting angry. Very angry. He wanted answers. He was beginning to feel that his town was *under attack*. Fortunately for him, Jilly and Mango's eye-witness accounts contained some very important clues.

'The cow moved through the air in an arc, you say?'

'Yes,' said Jilly Cheeter.

'Like a ball flying through the air –' added Mango Claptrap.

'As though it had been thrown?' asked the chief of police.

'Exactly!' the pair said together.

An image popped into Jilly's head: it was from a visit to Leftover Castle just outside Gimlet. She thought that the castle itself was a bit of a let down. It is one of those ancient ruins that is so ruined that you need a really good imagination to picture it as a building, let alone a castle. There aren't even any proper walls left, just clusters of stones here and there, with faded weather-proof notices next to them trying to get visitors excited. One of these notices, about the castle under attack, has a picture of a kind of giant wooden catapult – or slingshot – on wheels. It was this image that now flashed through Jilly Cheeter's mind.

'You don't think the cows were catapulted do you?' she gasped.

Grabby Hanson smiled a smile. 'That's

exactly what I'm thinking, young lady!' he said.

'But don't you think someone might – er – notice someone loading up a giant catapult?' she said.

Mango Claptrap started hopping on one leg and then the other with excitement. 'Not,' he said, 'if it was fired from out at sea!'

Grabby Hanson froze.

His good-looking chief-of-police face broke into an even bigger smile.

He then grabbed

Mango, lifted him up off the ground and hugged him. Then he hurriedly put him down again.

'Sorry about that,' he said, his face reddening. 'I got a bit emotional for a moment. You, Master Claptrap, are a *genius*. There was no need for gliders or hot-air balloons! The cows must have been fired from a vessel off the coast.'

'But why?' asked Jilly Cheeter, which, to my mind, was a very sensible question indeed.

'But who?' asked Mango Claptrap.

'*Why* and *who* are my job,' said Grabby Hanson, 'made all the easier now that we know *how*. I'll see to it that you both get gold medals the size of frying pans once all of this is over!'

Jilly and Mango glowed with pride, then Mango slipped over in a patch of jelly trifle.

Chapter Eight
The long arm of the law

The *who* and the *why* may have been Grabby Hanson's job, but do you think that stopped Jilly Cheeter and Mango Claptrap switching from watching the sky to watching the sea? Of course it didn't. Every chance they got they were looking out over the water in the hope of seeing . . . what? Someone with a giant catapult firing cows? Whatever it might be, they had their eyes glued to the sea, but with no success. The most exciting thing they saw was Mrs Awning fall off the ferry.

Again.

Then, a few days later, news reached town that Grabby Hanson had got his man. And woman. And children.

Jilly Cheeter heard the news from Premix Stipend, whose body hums all the time as though she's hiding a jar of angry bees up her jumper. She wasn't always like that. Her troubles date back to when Chevvy Offal (of Offal's Sunbeds) had put her in one of his sunbeds as a last-minute appointment then, forgetting all about her, had locked up shop and gone to an extraordinary town meeting.

Offal's sunbeds in Offal's Sunbeds are rather like giant sandwich-toasters with pull-down lids. And these lids can't be pushed up by the person inside, which is probably how Offal got all six of them so cheap. When Miss Stipend was discovered the following morning, her skin was the colour of gravy, her hair was a crispy black – and fell out when touched – and her body was humming the hum. Over time, her hair grew back and her skin turned a more pleasant orange, but the humming remains.

Jilly was in The Rusty Dolphin drinking a can of **Drooly Slurp** through a red see-through bendy straw when Miss Stipend burst in with the news.

'Grabby Hanson's made an arrest!' she declared to anyone who would listen (which was everyone in the place). 'Out on the water.'

There was a murmur of excitement and the scraping of chairs as people got to their feet and piled out into the sunlight. Jilly was amongst those who then lined the jetty to watch Grabby Hanson bringing his police launch alongside, towing a small fishing trawler behind him.

On the deck of the police launch was Constable Gelatine with a handcuffed Derek Fox on one side of him and a handcuffed

Bunty Fox on the other. Behind them was a
fishing net containing what later turned out
to be Shaun, Mantle, Fastbuck and Garrideb
Fox, all in a terrible tangle. The launch was
towing a fishing trawler. Attached to the
winch at the back of the trawler, designed to

raise and lower the fishing nets, was an
enormous homemade slingshot in which
nestled a life-size model cow, smaller but
otherwise identical to those which had
landed on Purple Outing's Music Shack and
in Minty Glibb's giant part-made jelly trifle.

The crowd on the jetty burst into applause. There were wolf-whistles, cheers and cries.

Jilly wished that Mango was there to see this, so she dashed off to find him.

Once on land (and after some serious untangling) the six Foxes were led away towards a battered old police van which was parked nearby. Mum and Dad Fox – Bunty and Derek – held their heads high and even shouted a few odd slogans along the lines of, 'Kill all ducks!' and 'A fair scoop is a full scoop!' Their teenage children looked more sheepish and generally embarrassed all round.

The Grubtown police department wasn't used to dealing with so many arrests at once, so didn't have enough handcuffs for the younger Foxes. Grabby Hanson sent Constable Gelatine off to the general store which sells just about anything and everything from wax lips to toy handcuffs 'with real keys'. Gelatine soon returned with a brown paper bag.

'Did you get a receipt, Sergeant?' Grabby asked him. (Constable Gelatine is a sergeant, remember. The 'Constable' part is just his name.)

'Yes, Chief,' nodded the sergeant. He took the toy handcuffs out of their yellow cardboard-backed wrapping (putting the rubbish back into the paper bag) and proceeded to snap them round the remaining Foxes' wrists.

'Ices should be nice!' shouted Mr Fox.

'Reasonable ices at reasonable prices!' shouted Mrs Fox. She tried to struggle free from Grabby's firm grasp and somehow managed to kick the bag from Gelatine's hand.

Pieces of torn yellow cardboard and see-through plastic scattered everywhere.

The crowd gasped.

'Add littering to the charges,' said Grabby Hanson to no one in particular, just to let the Foxes know that they were getting into deeper and deeper trouble by the minute.

Chapter Nine
A startling discovery

The gathered townsfolk booed and jeered and shook a fist or two (mostly their own) at the Foxes. Back then, the Foxes were probably the least-liked folk in Grubtown apart, of course, from Wide Brim Petty-Mandrake. (If you're thinking, 'Why *of course*?' then you obviously don't know Wide Brim Petty-Mandrake.)

When the last of the Foxes – Fastbuck – was in the back of the battered police van and Constable Gelatine had slammed the doors and turned the handle, people began to drift away. (You could just make out Derek shouting something like 'We dream of fresh cream!' from inside.)

Luminous Shard stood on the jetty scratching his bald head. He looked at the fishing boat with its slingshot and the latest life-size model cow. And tried to make sense of it all.

Mango Claptrap, meanwhile, was less than eight minutes away from finding himself in an adventure of his very own. At about the same time that Jilly and the customers at The Rusty Dolphin had been alerted to what was happening by Premix Stipend, he had gone to the newsagent's to pick up an extra special mega-bumper three-issues-in-one word-search puzzle book which his dad had had on order for over a month. After collecting and paying for it (and buying half a bag of Trimble's Penny Chews with the change), he headed for his house.

Mango Claptrap never took the most obvious way home. He liked to go through the more interesting parts of Grubtown, which included the river walk that ran along the bottom of the garden of what had once been the home of TV chef Hybrid Byword.

A bit further on, he came to the big stretch

of land where there was the secret door to the caverns where Hybrid Byword had secretly stored his fabulous stash of fabulous pudding. The nettles and scrub had long since been cleared, and a much much bigger opening, covered with a large metal door, had been installed so that cranes could lift out slabs of the pudding in huge containers. All the pudding was now long gone, and the door was always padlocked and bolted.

Only now it wasn't.

To Mango Claptrap's complete and utter jaw-dropping and smacking-of-gob amazement, it was lying open.

W I D E O P E N.

And it seemed to be like a big mouth saying, 'Explore me!'

At that moment, a panting Jilly Cheeter appeared at his side. 'Found you!' she said triumphantly, gasping for breath. 'You'll never guess who was behind the catapulting cows.'

'Look,' said Mango, excitedly pointing at the open door.

Jilly looked. 'Wow,' she said. 'It's open.'

'Wide open.' Mango nodded.

'Were you about to –?'

'Yes.'

'Shall we –?'

'Yes.'

Neither was going to miss this once-in-a-lifetime opportunity. Mango clambered down the first few rungs of the rusty metal ladder, set into a wall of solid rock, and Jilly was quick to follow.

'Who was it who was catapulting the cows, then?' asked the shorts-clad Claptrap as they made their way down.

'The Fox family. All of them!'

'I should have known!' said Mango. 'They're so . . . so . . .'

'*Horrible*?' suggested Jilly Cheeter.

'That's the word!' agreed Mango Claptrap.

'Any idea why they did it?'

'None whatsoever,' said Jilly, 'but I've never understood the Foxes anyhow.'

'And I suppose there can never be a *good* reason for catapulting cows,' Mango Claptrap added wisely.

He slowed down then stopped, so Jilly — a few rusty rungs above him — had to do the same. Despite being so close to the river, the cave walls were dry and there were no sounds of dripping water, just an eerie silence.

'Dark,' said Mango.

'Very,' said Jilly.

They continued their climb down.

I don't know what it was that young Jilly Cheeter and Mango Claptrap expected to find when they reached the bottom of the ladder.

But

it

certainly

wasn't

Hybrid

Byword.

But there he was.

Chapter Ten
A fresh start

Hybrid Byword was half-sitting half-lying on the cavern floor, his back propped up against a rocky wall.

'You're Hybrid Byword!' said Mango in amazement, his words bouncing off the sides of the vast empty cavern in a chorus of echoes.

'Yup,' said Hybrid Byword with his trademark 'Yup'. He was wearing his trademark chef's hat that looked like a giant muffin. When he'd first worn it, his hat had made him stand out from all

other chefs. When he became WILDLY
POPULAR, copies of his hat sold by their
zillions so everyone was wearing them. But it
still looked best on him.

'You're dead,' said a stunned Jilly Cheeter,
the word 'dead' echoing, echoing, echoing.
'You died years ago!'

'Yup,' said Hybrid Byword with his
trademark repetition. (He was so famous and

so familiar that just about *everything* about him was a trademark something or other.)

'But . . . How? I mean . . .'

'My heart stopped at the hospital,' said Byword.

'That certainly sounds like – er – dying to me,' said Jilly.

'The hospital staff thought so,' agreed Hybrid Byword. 'They unplugged the pluggy things, switched off the bleepy things – which had stopped bleeping anyhow – and had a doctor sign a death certificate.'

'But you're not dead *now*,' said Jilly Cheeter.

'We can both see that,' said Mango Claptrap.

'Well, yes and no,' said Byword. 'I mean, my heart must have started beating again or I wouldn't be here, would I? But legally I'm dead. I even have a copy of the certificate to prove it.'

The world-famous dead chef reached inside his jacket pocket. It was an effort. He looked rather *crumpled*.

'We believe you,' said Mango. He paused. 'I hope you don't mind me asking, but where have you been all these years? I was really little when you – er – died.'

He still looked little to Hybrid Byword, especially in those short shorts, but the chef knew what he meant.

'I was very young too,' said Jilly, 'but I do remember the town funeral. It was a really big deal.'

'Hey, you weren't *there*, were you, Mr Byword?' asked Mango Claptrap. The idea of being at your own funeral seemed pretty cool to him.

'No.'

'Then where were you?' asked Jilly.

'When I realised that being dead might not be such a bad thing, I left Grubtown as soon as possible. I moved far, far away.'

'So who did they – er – bury?' asked Jilly.

'A coffin full of my rivals' cookbooks.' He laughed. 'Being a celebrity isn't all it's cracked up to be, you know. For a while, it was good to start afresh.'

'But you're back now,' said Mango, looking around. His eyes had got used to the dim light. He could make out a large kitchen area with an enormous double-door fridge, a huge cooking range and all sorts of pots and pans and whisks and gizmos. It looked very out of place in the vast, empty –

and rocky – surroundings.

'I'm back,' agreed Byword. He didn't look very comfortable.

Mango suddenly had a thought. 'You're not upset about your secret stash of pudding being found and sold are you?' he asked.

'Not in the slightest. I'm very happy for Purple.'

'Hey, you're not –?'

'Ronald Brown?' said Hybrid Byword, referring to the mysterious man who now lived in his mansion. 'Of course I am. I missed the old house, so it's good to be back living in it again, even if I am legally dead and living under a different name.'

'And under an extraordinary false beard,' Mango Claptrap added.

'And that,' Hybrid Byword nodded. 'It was my mother's.'

'This may seem a silly question, Mr Byword,' said Mango (who was very good at asking very *sensible* questions, as you may have noticed), 'but why are you telling us all of this? I mean, you went to all this trouble to pretend not to be you for all these years . . .'

'I was wondering that too,' said Jilly Cheeter (who'd been wondering that too).

'Because I'm dying,' said Hybrid Byword, 'which is a strange thing for a dead man to be doing.'

There was a short gap in the conversation.

It lasted from about **here**.

To about **here**.

But it somehow seemed much longer than it really was, and it was VERY silent. Mango Claptrap could just make out the sound of the nearby river through the cavern walls.

'Are you old or ill or something?' asked Jilly Cheeter with an unhappy mixture of real shock and real concern.

'All three,' said the world-famous TV chef.

'I'm pretty ancient, my heart's never been quite as good as it used to be since I died, and I fell off that ladder a few days ago. I've been here ever since.'

Jilly looked at Mango who was looking at her.

'I think I've done myself a serious injury,' said Byword. 'This time I really think it is the end of the road for me.'

Both Mango and Jilly had noticed Hybrid Byword had been sitting oddly. Now Mango felt a surge of panic. 'I'll go and get help!' he said.

'Please don't,' said Byword. 'I don't want a fuss.' It looked like he was about to add something further then decided not to.

'What is it?' asked Jilly Cheeter.

'I was wondering . . . there isn't a cow wandering about up there, is there, by any chance?' He looked up towards the square of daylight way, way above them.

'A cow?' gasped Mango.

'Is she black and white and very friendly?' asked Jilly Cheeter.

'That's her!' said Byword.

'No there isn't,' said Jilly.

Hybrid Byword frowned. 'Then how did you know — ?'

'But there *was*,' explained Jilly Cheeter. 'Just how many days have you been stuck down here, Mr Byword?'

'Three? Four? I've lost count.' The chef shrugged and winced with pain a little. 'Why?'

'It's just that your cow landed on Limbo Goulash a while back. It was big news,' Mango said. He went on to explain everything he knew.

When he'd finished, Jilly Cheeter supplied the ending: the arrest of the Fox family on their strangely converted fishing trawler.

'How extraordinary!' said Hybrid Byword.

'That's some story. It was my cow that got me into this mess. She escaped from my back garden one night and wandered off down to the river walk, and I went looking for her . . . and I fell through the doorway. I must have left it open.'

'You fell all the way down here?'

'I managed to grab the rungs of the ladder a few times to slow my fall,' said Byword, managing a grin, 'which is probably why one of my arms is now a little longer than the other. Look.'

He wasn't kidding.

Mango made up his mind. 'Now I'm going to get you that doctor,' he said. 'And you can't stop me.'

Byword looked down at his own legs. 'That's true,' he said.

★ ★ ★

As Mango was making his way back up the ladder and Jilly Cheeter was comforting the dead celebrity chef as best she could, Derek Fox was in the back of the police van, arguing that he knew his rights. 'I know my rights!' he said. 'We haven't done anything wrong.'

Chief of Police Grabby Hanson leaned around from the front passenger seat and glared at them through the grille. 'How would you like to be cycling along minding your own business and have a cow land on top of you?' he demanded, 'But, fortunately for you, Limbo Goulash seems none the worse for wear. Then there's the damage to Purple Outing's Music Shack,' he reminded them, 'but Purple can easily afford to repair it. Destroying Minty Glibb's attempt at a

world-beating jelly trifle was tragic, but she can try again. But catapulting a *live cow* from a fishing trawler —'

'We weren't aiming for —' began Mantle Fox.

'Don't admit to anything!' Bunty Fox ordered.

'I know my rights,' said Derek Fox.

'Whether the cow was fired directly at anyone on purpose or not, cruelty to animals is something that we've never taken to kindly in Grubtown,' Grabby Hanson reminded the proprietor of Kill All Ducks.

'No,' said Derek Fox in a meek little voice. 'It was an accident.'

Constable Gelatine, who was driving, snorted. 'How can anyone take a cow out on a boat and accidentally fire her from a slingshot?'

'It's a long story,' said Derek Fox.

'Then put it in your statement,' said Grabby Hanson.

So that's exactly what he did.

Chapter Eleven
In his own words

On Sundays, me, Bunty and the kids always go and have ice-creams at 'Cones' on Himble Street, near the old tree that always smells of dog. You know, opposite that candle shop which burnt down and the life-raft shop which sank when the water-main burst.

I like three big scoops in a knickerbocker glass with loads of raspberry sauce, and Bunty likes two scoops with chocolate sauce and sprinkle-spronkles. We call

them our 'Sunday sundaes', which is
what is called a play on words. We
often say clever stuff like that. We
have joke names for most of the losers
in town. Not you, Sergeant. Not that
you're a loser, of course.

Lately, we found the scoops of ice-
cream were getting smaller. They still
cost us the same but the scoops were
not as big. When I complained to Leggy
Prune, I mean Leggy Johnson, she said
that Wretching's Dairy (who own
'Cones') had given them new smaller
metal scoops to scoop out the ice-cream
with. I said that was cheating and that
the dairy should have kept the scoops
the same size but put the prices up.
That way customers would get the same
as before and know that they were
paying more for it. By keeping the

price the same but making the scoops
smaller they were trying to trick us,
and no one tries to trick the Fox
family and gets away with it.

No, sir.

I rang up Wretching's Dairy but they
wouldn't listen. We all wrote to the
local papers* but they wouldn't publish
any of our letters about it. They never
publish our letters any more and we
send them over fifty a week. Then I
spoke to Mr Petty-Mandrake who is good
when it comes to complaining, and he
suggested DIRECT ACTION.

We could not think what direct action
to take until my daughter Garrideb came
back with a cow she had found. It had
been wandering about on its own and

* *The Grubtown Daily Herald* and
The Grubtown Weekly Gerald

didn't seem to belong to anyone so
that's not stealing. Then I had one of
my smart ideas. We would make life-size
cows, which looked like the one in the
Wretching's Dairy logo, and bombard the
town with them MAKING EACH ONE SLIGHTLY
SMALLER THAN THE LAST, like the dairy
has done with the ice-cream scoop
sizes.

It would get the town talking. It would
be like a riddle.

'Where are these cows coming from?'

'Are they to do with the dairy in some
way?'

'Why are they SHRINKING???'

Then, once we had everyone's attention,

we could explain it was a protest about
the ice-cream PORTIONS shrinking. About
the scoops getting smaller.

Clever, no?

We used the cow my daughter found as a
model for our model cows. We copied her
shape and stuff and painted on the
markings to look like hers so that our
pretend cows looked as much like the
real cow as possible. We did all the
building and painting on the fishing
boat, away from nosy neighbours. We
also knew catapulting the cows from a
boat would make us much harder to find.
Only, the real cow got caught in the
catapult meant for the model cows and
somehow got catapulted by mistake.

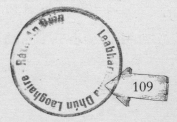

The statement went on for another few pages, with Mr Fox going out of his way to say how relieved he was that neither the cow nor poor old Limbo Goulash was seriously injured. His only other regret, he said, was that the cow hadn't landed on a group of ducks, 'killing them all outright'. No one doubted that part.

Chapter Twelve
Clap! Cheer! Hooray!

Once all six Foxes' statements had been (very neatly) typed up by Constable Gelatine, Grabby Hanson sat in his office (with its bricked-up window) and read through them, one after the other.

'I think they're telling the truth,' he said to Gelatine.

'I think they're nuts,' said his sergeant. 'All those years of hating the Grubtown ducks has made them weird and twisted inside.'

'That's true,' Grabby agreed. 'Anyway, I think that just about wraps it up. All we need now is a nice trial and for the mayor to present medals to the Cheeter girl and the Claptrap boy for their invaluable assistance.' Flabby Gomez loves awarding medals. Often to himself.

The two policeman were interrupted by a knock on the open office door.

Dr Fraud leaned around the doorway into the room. 'You'll never guess who I've just patched up, Chief,' he said.

'Who?'

'Hybrid Byword.'

'But he's dead.'

'Not in the living breathing sense, he isn't,' said Dr Fraud. 'But he has had a bit of a nasty fall, and I need you to help me get him out.'

'Out?' asked Grabby Hanson. 'Out of where?'

'Follow me,' said Dr Fraud, 'and bring plenty of rope.'

★ ★ ★

So there you have it. Now you know who was behind the falling cows (those dastardly Foxes), and that the live one landing on Limbo Goulash really *had* been a freak accident (which was why I called it a freak accident in the first place). As to why Hybrid Byword had wanted a cow, it was for his latest cookery experiments: milk puddings like you wouldn't believe. He wasn't only back from the dead and back in Grubtown but he was also *back in the kitchen*. He'd bought the cow off the Internet from a retiring farmer who'd had her delivered one night away from prying eyes.

Jilly Cheeter and Mango Claptrap got their medals as promised, at a special ceremony in the town hall. Though not quite as big as your average frying pan, the medals would have put a small saucepan to shame. Grabby Hanson made a speech, Mayor Flabby Gomez made a speech and even Hybrid Byword made a speech (from his wheelchair, having been pushed on to the

stage by Dr Fraud for very little extra charge). There was an awkward moment when both medals were found to be missing from their purple crushed-velvet-lined presentation cases, but Grabby Hanson managed to track them down. (To inside his jacket.)

Mango's dad, Furl Claptrap, was there in the audience, sitting proudly at the front, his

head buried in a word-search puzzle for 'different types of furniture'. Next to him sat Mango's mum, Carport Claptrap, who was beaming proudly and not for one moment taking her eyes off her son up on stage. Mango's brother, Vestige, however, had a finger up his nose – in true Big Man Gomez style – and seemed more interested in his own shoes. Jilly's father, Sloop Cheeter, was proudly watching from up in the balcony. He wasn't up at the front because he'd managed to sneak in Harvey their dog, despite the handwritten notice on the entrance to the town hall which read:

NO Dogs, and that includes the Cheeters' dog Harvey

Sloop had smuggled him in under his coat, which he had to keep on despite it being a very hot day. He considered the dog a member of the family and wasn't going to let him miss such an important Cheeter event if he could help it. When Flabby Gomez pinned the medal to Jilly Cheeter's T-shirt, Harvey barked in delight. For some reason, everyone seemed to think that it had been Camshaft Thrift, owner of THE RUSTY DOLPHIN, who'd made the noise and he was thrown out on to the street by town hall officials.

I was there in the audience as well, of course. I sat in the very back row because, being so tall, people behind me often complain that my head is in the way. Being a little chunky – rather than weedy and thin – people often complain that the *rest* of me is in the way too. (It's all muscle, you know.) I got a few funny looks. Some folk are jealous of my splendid beard.

As for Hybrid Byword, he had risen from the dead and, eventually, made a full recovery from his fall. This was big news. This was

HUGE news. This was *international* news. This was incredible. Hybrid Byword was back.

No wonder none of us will forget that time in Grubtown: the year that it rained cows.

THE END

This Way Please!

Another word from Beardy Ardagh

When I tell people about events in Grubtown, they usually ask why so many of the townsfolk 'have such silly names'. The obvious answer might be to say, 'ARE YOU TALKING TO ME? DO YOU HAVE AN APPOINTMENT?' but what I actually do is ask: 'What's so silly about them?'

I've said it before, and I'll say it again: don't forget that the man who first drew Mickey Mouse in films went by the name of Ub Iwerks – not Walt Disney – and people didn't laugh and point at *him*. 'Silly' is in the eye – sometimes the left eye and sometimes the right – of the beholder.

If, for some ridiculous reason, you'd like to write to me about **GRuBtoWN taLes**, please address the envelope:

Beardy Ardagh,
c/o Faber & Faber,
Bloomsbury House
74–77 Great Russell Street,
London,
WC1B 3DA

and write **Grubtown TaLes** in the bottom left–hand corner. **DON'T FORGET TO INCLUDE A STAMPED SELF-ADDRESSED ENVELOPE** if you're hoping for a reply. Not that I can promise you'll get one. I have a beard to comb, bread to spread, and books to write. I'm a busy man!

(Just some of) the folk who pop up in GRuBtoWN taLes

Jilly Cheeter girl and one-time duck-gatherer

Mango Claptrap a short boy in short trousers, whatever the weather

Manual Org a smoothy skinned fellow

Flabby Gomez Mayor of Grubtown

Kumquat 'Grabby' Hanson the chief of police

The Grumbly girls the seven Grumbly daughters

Hacking-Cough Gomez the mayor's brother

Big Man Gomez the mayor's dead dad

Pritt Gomez the mayor's wife

Tundra Gomez the mayor's son and heir

Formal Dripping official village idiot for the nearby village of Werty

Derek, Bunty, Shaun, Mantle, Fastbuck & Garrideb Fox the duck-hating Fox family of humans (not foxes)

Rambo Sanskrit council job-giver-outer

Sonia Pipkin local builder

The troll inhabitant of Beardy Ardagh's airing cupboard

Mrs Awning town accident-waiting-to-happen, first name unknown

Minty Glibb owner of Minty's Cake Shop

Mickey 'Steamroller' Johnson doughnut-loving steamroller driver

Leggy Prune the future Mrs Johnson

Mrs Johnson the former Leggy Prune

Constable Gelatine a police sergeant

Mustard Tripwire an officer of the law and
Gelatine's nephew

Galaxy Tripwire a train driver and former
beauty queen

Relish Tripwire a tropical fish salesperson

Informative Boothe a very knowledgeable chap

Hobo Browne a gentleman of the road/smelly
tramp

Camshaft Thrift owner of The Rusty Dolphin
Cafe

Farflung Heaps self-appointed leader of an
angry mob

Garlic Hamper the lighthouse keeper

Shoona Loose the world-famous singer who
does a lot for animal charities

Tawdry Hipbone movie star

Snooks Miss Hipbone's pampered pooch

Luminous Shard bald heckler and mechanic

Carlo Monte the riverboat gambler

Lefty Scorn proprietor of Scorn's Laundrette
& Jeweller's

Acrid Scorn an irresponsible dumper of
hazardous waste

Jip the town pelican (official mascot)

Marley Gripe a painter of signs

Dr Fraud a pretend doctor (but he's cheap)

Sloop Cheeter Jilly's dad

Harvey the Cheeter family dog

Furl Claptrap Mango's dad

Carport Claptrap Mango's mum

Vestige Claptrap Mango's brother

Claws their cat

Partial Coggs Grubtown's resident artist

Slackjaw Gumshoe paint & hardware store owner

Purple Outing very rich owner of Purple Outing's Music Shack

Hind-Leg Outing amongst other things, mother of Purple's vast number of children

Wide Brim Petty-Mandrake a regular complainer

Hetty Glue-Pen cinema manager and projectionist

Condo Blotch former cleaner now head of her very own keep-fit and health-food empire

Emily Blotch Condo's daughter

Free-Kick leader of the escaped lab rats

Lulu Free-Kick's mate for life

Paltry Feedback a printer and cake decorator

Careworn Wormwood nine-day king of Grubtown

Glowering Silt general manager of Fettle's hotel

Avid Folklore manager of Fettle's hotel

Chevvy Offal owner of Offal's Sunbeds

Premix Stipend victim of one of Offal's sunbeds

Hybrid Byword the (now dead) TV chef

Limbo Goulash an office worker

Clam Wretching founder of Wretching's Dairy

Barton Wretching her son and current owner of the dairy

Beardy Ardagh honoured citizen of Grubtown and the teller of these tales

The delightful Beardy Ardagh tells of other GRuBtoWN taLes

If you promise to leave me alone, I'll tell you about some of the other Grubtown Tales, as long as you tell EVERY (THIRD) PERSON YOU MEET TODAY about them. (And make sure that they have a library card or enough money to buy a book or two.) It goes without saying that they are all excellent – the **GRuBtoWN taLes**, not every (third) person you meet – and that Jilly Cheeter and Mango Claptrap turn up in them somewhere. If you find any spelling mistakes or other errors in the books, it's not my fault. (It's other people's job to spot them.) If you like the books, however, IT'S ALL THANKS TO ME.

Now read on . . .

GRuBtoWN taLes

Book One

Stinking Rich aNd Just PlaiN StiNky

or

A Diamond As Big As His Head

Grubtown is full of oddballs — from the singing Grumbly girls to a family of duck-haters, and an out-sized mayor who's knitting a new house — but Manual Org is too repulsive even for them. Getting him to leave town is top priority, until the discovery of a humongous diamond changes everything.

YOU SHOULD HAVE READ THIS ONE ALREADY!

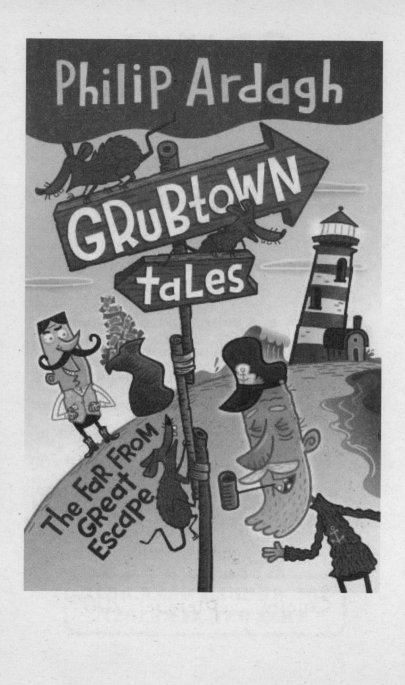

GRuBtoWN taLes

Book Three

The FaR FRoM GReat EscaPe

or

The Light, the Swith and the Wardrobe

When the local lighthouse is plunged into darkness and a ship runs aground – flattening The Rusty Dolphin – it's hard to imagine things can get much worse in Grubtown. But then there's a jailbreak and the police department (all three of them) needs all the help it can get from the (often bonkers) townsfolk. No wonder more trouble is waiting just around the corner.

Coming SePtembeR 2009

AT A LOOSE END?

Visit

Win stuff – great competitions each month.

Have your say – join the kidszone panel and have your say about your likes, dislikes and what you've been reading.

Play games – visit our microsites and play our addictive games Nut Ding, Manic Mundi and The Parliament of Blood. More coming soon!

More stuff – read extracts from our latest books, listen to audio clips, find out about your favourite authors and much more.

It's all at:

www.faberkids.co.uk

Just read a Faber book? Let us know what you think. Send your review to kidszone@faber.co.uk. Your review might feature on the website and will be entered for our review of the month competition.